What Shall We Play Now?

Written and translated by

Taghreed A. Najjar

Illustrated by

Charlotte Shama

Crocodile Books, USA
An imprint of Interlink Publishing Group, Inc.
www.interlinkbooks.com

My Mama is a seamstress.
When ladies carrying beautiful pieces of cloth come to our house,
Mama takes their measurements with her measuring tape.
She marks the cloth with a piece of soap, cuts it with a pair
of scissors, then sews it with a needle and thread.
Clickety clank, clickety clank, goes our old sewing machine.

My Mama is always, always busy.
Sometimes I hold the pin box for her.
Other times I fold pieces of cloth or
fetch her the measuring tape.

One day my Mama gave me a piece of cloth.
It was soft as silk, green as grass,
and cool as a breeze.

I thought and thought...
What can I do with a piece of
cloth? What can I do?

Then... with a **flick** and a **click**,
in just a **blink**, with **no magic stick**,
I became a superhero.

I ran here, I ran there. I flew high up in the sky.
I swooped down to save people from dangers near and far.

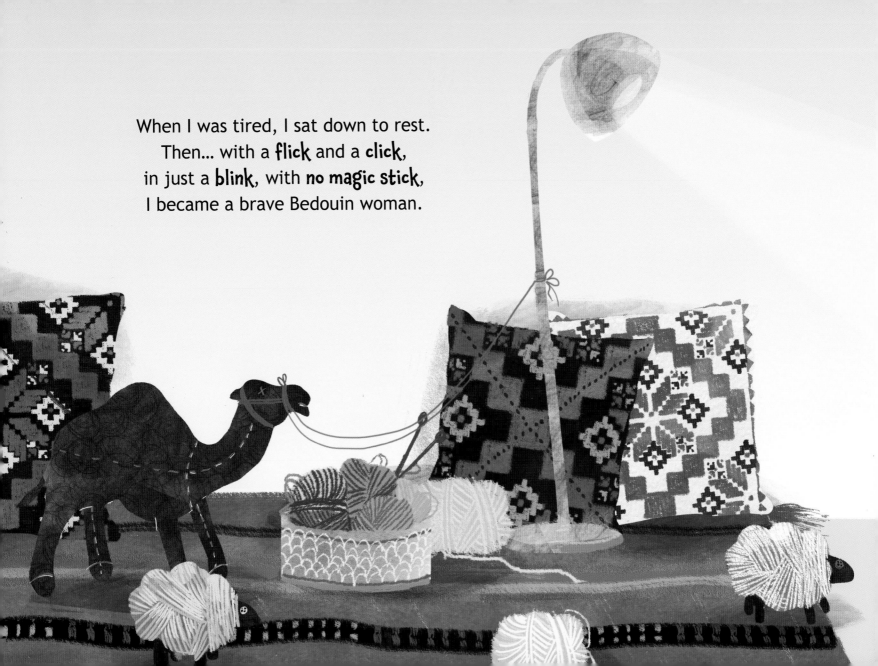

When I was tired, I sat down to rest.
Then... with a **flick** and a **click**,
in just a **blink**, with **no magic stick**,
I became a brave Bedouin woman.

I led caravans of camels.
I herded my sheep to an oasis deep and
was not afraid of big bad wolves.

My friend Raya came to visit me.
She said, "I'm bored. What can we play?"
I answered her excitedly,
"My Mama gave me a piece of cloth.
It is as green as grass, as soft as silk,
as cool as a breeze."

Raya laughed out loud and said, "Are you serious? Do you want us to play with a piece of cloth?"

"Yes, just close your eyes," I said.
Then... with a **flick** and a **click**,
in just a **blink**, with **no magic stick**,
Raya became a princess. I said to her, "Let's pretend,
Raya. You are a princess, and I am your loyal subject."

Raya and I played all afternoon
with the green piece of cloth.
First, I became a butterfly.
I flew over colorful fields and
sipped the nectar from flowers.

Then Raya became a Maharaja.
She held a golden scepter and ruled the lands that lay between
the mountains of India and the plains of Pakistan.

Then... with a **flick** and a **click**,
in just a **blink**, with **no magic stick**,
I became a Roman soldier.
I carried a long spear and
battled a lion so fierce.

Raya said, "What else can we play?"
I thought and thought.
Then... with a **flick** and a **click**,
in just a **blink**, with **no magic stick**,
the piece of cloth became a baby doll.

We called her Mira.
Raya said, "I am the Papa."
I said, "I am the Mama."
We fed our little girl,
cuddled her, and sang her a lullaby.

♪ Mira, Mira, ♪
Sweet and gentle Mira
Sleep now, sleep, ♪
In your soft bed, sleep. ♪

Raya jumped up and down, saying, "It's my turn now! It's my turn!"
Then... with a **flick** and a **click**, in just a **blink**, with **no magic stick**,
Raya became a hula dancer from Hawaii.
Her long skirt swished gracefully from side to side as she swayed.

"What shall we play now?
Oh, what shall we play?"
Raya and I thought and thought.
Then we tied the green piece of cloth to a stick,
and with a **flick** and a **click**, in just a **blink**,
we were on Sinbad's sailing ship.
We sailed the oceans of faraway dreams.
We looked for pirate treasure in the deep blue sea,
singing our sailor song.

Hayla ya, hayla,
hayla, hayla.

Soon our bellies began to rumble with hunger.
Raya and I looked at each other and smiled.
Then... with a **flick** and a **click**,
in just a **blink**, with **no magic stick**,
the green piece of cloth became a tent.
We sat in its shade and drank juice and ate frosted cupcakes.
Mmm, those cakes were delicious.

Our neighbor came to visit Mama.
When she saw the green piece of cloth
she nodded her head and said,
"This sure is a nice big piece of cloth.
It will make a good tablecloth."

Raya and I burst out laughing and said,
"If only you knew, Auntie, if only you knew
**This piece of cloth is good for many
other things, too.**"

First published in 2022 by

Crocodile Books
An imprint of Interlink Publishing Group, Inc.
46 Crosby Street
Northampton, Massachusetts 01060
www.interlinkbooks.com

Originally published in Arabic by Al Salwa Publishers

Library of Congress Cataloging-in-Publication Data available
ISBN 978-1-62371-809-1

2 4 6 8 10 9 7 5 3 1

Printed and bound in Korea